LITTLE CRITTER®

FALL STORYBOOK COLLECTION

BY MERCER MAYER

This Book Belongs to:

_____

LITTLE CRITTER®
FALL STORYBOOK COLLECTION

BY MERCER MAYER

HARPER
An Imprint of HarperCollinsPublishers

Table of Contents

THE FALL FESTIVAL

It is fall.

The leaves change colors.

They turn yellow and red.

We are driving in the car.

We drive to the Fall Festival.

Lots of critters are there.

We bring a wagon
to hold the things we buy.

13

I see so many apples.

I try one.

Mom pays the man.

Little Sister has apple cider.

She spills it.

It is sticky.

We go on a hayride.

There is not much hay.

We ride through
a field full of pumpkins.

17

I watch a critter
shoot pumpkins into the air.
They go SPLAT!

It is fun to watch.

We walk to the apple trees.
I see critters picking apples.

I get to pick apples, too.

Dad buys the apples that we pick.

Mom will make many apple pies.

Yum! I eat another apple.

Mom says, "No more apples."

Next we look for
a Halloween pumpkin.

Some pumpkins are too small.

24

Some pumpkins
are too funny looking.

I find the perfect pumpkin.

It is big.

Mom finds
the perfect pumpkin, too.
It is not so big.

We play the horseshoe game.

We each get three throws.

We can win prizes.

I go first.

PRIZES

TRY YOUR LUCK

HIT ME!

RECYCLE HERE

29

I aim.

I throw.

I fly. Whoops!

I forgot to let go.

Dad goes next.

He wins every time.

He wins a bunny
for Little Sister
and a bear for me.

It is time to go home.

Little Sister pulls the wagon.

I help her.

Dad carries the pumpkin.
Mom picks up the apples
that we drop.

I think fall is great,

but I ate too many apples.

JUST A BIG STORM

A storm was coming. We saw dark
clouds and lightning in the distance.

"Let's check the weather channel," said Mom.

The weather critter said, "A big storm with lightning, rain, and hail will pass right over Critterville."

"We better get ready for anything," Dad said.
"We may lose power." Dad checked all the flashlights.

Little Sister and I
got water in buckets
for the toilet.

We put up a sign that read,
"Remember: Pour water in tank
before you flush."

We filled up pots at the sink for drinking water.
We put a sign on the fridge: "Do not open."

Then we rescued stuff from our yard.
The wind began to blow. It blew harder and
harder. It began to rain, too.

I saw our neighbor's garbage can fly right past our window.

Suddenly, the power went out. It was getting dark and we couldn't turn on a light.

Mom and Dad got out our battery-powered lanterns,
and everyone had their very own flashlight.

The wind was cold, so Dad built
a fire in the woodstove. We made
knots out of newspaper to start
the fire.

We found an old phone in the closet and plugged
it into the wall. Did you know old phones work
sometimes when you have no power?

I called some of my friends. They didn't have
any power either. I asked Mom and Dad if I could
have everyone come over for a sleepover.

Mom and Dad said, "No."
That didn't seem fair.

We baked potatoes in the woodstove and made grilled cheese with a pie iron. I was careful and didn't touch the hot stove.

52

We played board games by lantern light.
"This is just like camping," I said.

We got sleeping bags and all slept on the living room floor. Dad told ghost stories.

There was lots of thunder and lightning. I wasn't scared. I snuggled real close to Mom, just in case.

We couldn't sleep.
Mom read a book to us.
Dad fell asleep first.

56

When we woke up, our power was back on.
We saw the power company critters
working on the electrical poles.
That was neat.

I was sad that it was all over, but
Mom and Dad were happy. They
said they wanted to take showers.
Why would they want to do that?

Our phone rang. It was Grandma and Grandpa.
They were worried about us.

"Grandma, it wasn't so bad," I said.
"It was just a big storm."

GOING TO THE FIREHOUSE

Today my class is going
to the firehouse!
I dress like a fireman.
Time to fight a fire!

This is Fireman Joe.

This is his dog, Sparky.

Sparky is a fire dog.

Fireman Joe has boots.

He has a jacket.

He has a helmet.

I have boots.

I have a jacket.

I do not have a helmet.

Joe slides down the pole.
Sparky howls.
That is what he does
when there is a fire.

We see a fire truck.

It is big.

It is red.

It has hoses and a ladder.

Joe checks the hoses.

He lets me help.

Whoosh goes the water.

This hose is working fine.

Joe checks the ladder.

He goes up and up.

He is in the sky.

Hello, Fireman Joe!

Joe checks the siren.

It goes Ooo! Eee! Ooo!

The siren is very loud.

I cover my ears.

Joe tells us about fires.

He tells us smoke goes up.

When smoke goes up,
we must go down to the floor.

78

I get on the floor.

Joe tells us what to do if we are on fire.

Stop,

drop,

and roll!

I stop, drop, and roll!

Fireman Joe smiles.

He has a surprise.

He reaches into his truck.

Helmets for everyone!

I put on my helmet.

Joe tells me I will be
a good fireman one day.

Ding! Ding! goes the fire alarm.

I wave good-bye to Fireman Joe.

I wave good-bye to Sparky.

Time to fight a fire!

87

Fireman Joe is ready to go!
Sparky is, too.

THE BEST SHOW
& SHARE

"Next week is show and share, so figure out what to bring," my teacher said.

The bell rang. It was time to go home. She gave us a sheet of paper for our parents to sign.

At home, I asked Mom, "What can I bring?"

"Bring your dog," she said.

Little Sister wanted me to bring her. "I can't bring you. You're my sister!" I said.

"So?" she said.

"Never mind," I said, and went outside.

Maybe I could bring an ant farm.
No, ants are too yucky.

Maybe I could collect different leaves.
No, too much work.

I called my friends. Timothy was bringing his tarantula. Tiger was bringing his long-haired hamster named Thundercloud. Henrietta was bringing her dog, Fluffy.

Gator was bringing his stamp collection.
Malcom was bringing his snake. Bun Bun
was bringing her doll collection.

I didn't know what to bring. I went to the
stream to find some worms for fishing.

I was looking around when a big
bullfrog hopped out of the stream
right into my coffee can for worms!
Wow, that's great, I thought.

I put the lid on the can and took
the bullfrog home.

Dad found an old aquarium.
We fixed it up for my frog.

99

We put him in, but before we got the lid on, he jumped out right across the room into the coffee can on the floor.

"Wow," said Dad. "He likes that can!"

100

We tried again and he did the same thing over and over again.

"You've got a special show and share," said Mom.

I named him Leaping Lizard.

I told my friends about Leaping Lizard
but they didn't believe me. After school, I
showed them and they were amazed.

I made a poster all about bullfrogs. I got pictures off the Internet. The night before show and share, I pasted everything down. Leaping Lizard sat in his coffee can watching me. He really liked that can!

I went to bed so excited about the next day.
Morning came and I jumped out of bed, got
dressed, and ate breakfast. All the parents
were driving their kids to school that day.

I went to get my frog. He was gone! Oh, no!
I forgot to put the top on his aquarium. I ran
to the coffee can. No frog.

"Mom!" I screamed. "Leaping Lizard is missing!"
We looked everywhere.

I was already late for school.

Mom said, "Take your poster to share. I'll give you a note for the teacher. I'm sure I will find your frog."

We went to school. I was so upset. Everyone took turns showing and sharing. When it was my turn, I thought I would be sick.

Suddenly, Mom came into the room with
the aquarium, the coffee can, and my frog.
"I found him!" she said.

I took my turn. Everyone was amazed. Leaping Lizard jumped into the can every time. When it was all over, I got the "Most Interesting" ribbon.

Malcom was mad because he thought
his snake should win.

Timothy got "Most Scary." Henrietta's dog got
"Most Fluffy." Actually, everyone got a ribbon.
It was the best show and share ever!

SNOWBALL SOUP

I am Little Critter.

This is Little Sister.

She is my little sister.

That is Dog.

He is our dog.

Wow! Look at all the snow!

Dog likes snow.

Little Sister likes snow.

I like snow, too.

We play in the snow.

I dig in the snow.

Little Sister rolls in the snow.

We make snowballs.

We throw snowballs.

Oops!

Sorry, Little Sister.

We make a snowman.

We roll some big snowballs.

One, two, three.

One snowball on the bottom.

The next one goes on top.

This one goes on the very top.

Ta-da!

Little Sister puts on the hat.

I put on the nose.

Dog puts on the arms.

Then we put on the eyes.

Hello, Snowman!

Time for lunch, Snowman!

What does a snowman eat?

Snowball soup!
We make a pot of
snowball soup.

We give the snowman a spoon.
Eat all your soup, Snowman!

131

We go inside.

We eat soup for lunch, too!

Yum! Yum!

Thank you, Mom!

We go outside.

Oh, no! Dog is eating
the snowball soup.

Silly dog!

Snowball soup is not for dogs.

That was for the snowman.

Don't worry, Snowman!

Time to make more
snowball soup.
Yum! Yum!

THE LOST DINOSAUR BONE

Our class went on a field trip to the Museum of Natural History. I couldn't wait to see the dinosaurs. When I grow up, I'm going to be a dinosaur hunter.

But when we got to the museum, the
dinosaur exhibit was closed.

So, we had to see the butterflies instead. The butterflies were fun, but I really wished we could see the dinosaurs.

Next, we went to the Rain Forest. There were lots
of trees with monkeys in them.

"*Oooh! Oooh!*" I said to the monkeys.

A guard came running over to see the monkeys, too, so I asked him about the dinosaurs. I found out that the exhibit was closed because a Triceratops bone was missing!

In the Hall of Gems and Minerals it was very dark,
so we had to wear miner hats with lights on them.
Tiger went looking for diamonds, but I was busy
looking for the missing dinosaur bone. No luck!

After that, we went to the Planetarium, where the ceiling turned into a sky filled with stars.

We found out that the planet Mars is covered with dust and that the planet Saturn has rings around it.

I kept my eye out for the dinosaur bone, but I didn't see it.

On our way to see a meteorite, I asked Miss Kitty if I
could get a drink of water.

When I found the fountain, I also found something
else—the dinosaur exhibit! It had a big sign saying
EXHIBIT CLOSED.

I went closer and saw a Tyrannosaurus
rex. It was heading right for me!

I ran away as fast as I could . . .

. . . and found myself face-to-face with a Velociraptor.
It had its mouth open wide so I could see all its sharp,
pointy teeth.

The guard told me the exhibit was closed because of the missing dinosaur bone.

"I know," I said. "I've been looking for it everywhere."

On my way out, I took a wrong turn. That's when I saw something long and white sticking out from under the Ankylosaurus skeleton. It was the missing dinosaur bone!

I ran back to tell the guard.
He didn't believe me at first . . .

. . . but when I
showed the bone to
him, he gave me this
big smile.

Then I told Miss Kitty, and the guard took our whole class to the special place where the scientists who study dinosaur bones work.

"Thank you for solving the mystery of the missing Triceratops bone," the scientists told me.

160

Boy, were they happy to have that bone back, and so was Triceratops, the dinosaur the bone belonged to.

The scientists took us on a tour of the dinosaur exhibit. They showed us a Stegosaurus skeleton they had found buried in a mountain.

"I'm going to be a dinosaur hunter when I grow up!" I said.

"You already are," answered the scientists.

You know what I'm going to do tomorrow?
Dig for dinosaur bones in my backyard!

JUST CRITTERS WHO CARE

I play ball at Tiger's house.

I hit the ball very hard.

The ball flies next door.

Uh-oh! The ball is in the spooky yard.

Maybe a monster lives there.

I am brave.

I will get the ball.

I run.

I trip and fall.

A little old bunny

hands me our ball.

"Thank you," I say.

"Tiger, there's no monster there," I say.

I ask my dad
why it looks so spooky
at the old bunny's house.

"Mrs. Bunny is not feeling well.

She has no one to help her," Dad says.

"We can help Mrs. Bunny.
We are critters who care," I say.

I call my friends.

"What a great idea.

We will help, too," they say.

I make a picture for T-shirts.

Little Sister helps.

Dad gets them made.

We meet at my house.

Everyone wears a T-shirt.

Parents come, too.

We all walk

to Mrs. Bunny's house.

I knock on the door.

Mrs. Bunny says, "Hello."

"We are Critters Who Care!

May we help you
with your yard?" I ask.
"Thank you," says Mrs. Bunny.

183

We clip the bushes.

We cut the grass.

We pull up weeds.

We trim the trees.

Dad fixes the porch step.

Tiger's dad fixes the shutter.

I blow away old leaves.

The house and yard look great!

Mrs. Bunny brings cookies
and juice for all.
I help carry them.

189

We say good-bye.

"What should we do next?"

I ask.

190

Little Sister says, "We can
get toys for kids
who don't have any."

Everyone says, "Good idea!"

WeGOS

Wel

WeGO□AndSoo

WOG

WeGO✗✗AndSouP.✗□ ▓

is YumYum